Which Witch's Wand Works?

www.MyWorthwhileBooks.com

ISBN: 978-1-60010-500-5

12 11 10 09 1 2 3 4 5

Text copyright © 2004 by Meadowside Children's Books. Illustrations copyright © 2004 by Poly Bernatene.
First American edition, Worthwhile Books, 2009.

Published by arrangement with Meadowside Children's Books, 185 Fleet Street, London EC4A 2HS.

Worthwhile Books, a division of Idea and Design Works, LLC.
Editorial offices: 5080 Santa Fe Street, San Diego, CA 92109.
Printed in Korea.

Worthwhile Books does not read or accept unsolicited submissions of ideas, stories, or artwork.

Jonas Publishing, Publisher: Howard Jonas
IDW, President: Ted Adams
IDW, Senior Graphic Artist: Robbie Robbins

&

JONAS PUBLISHING

PRESENT:

WORTHWHILE
B O O K S

This is a story about
a witch called Rattle,
a witch called Ricket,
and their cat (called Rummy).

This is Rattle.
(She has trouble flying
in very strong winds.)

Every Friday evening, Rattle, Ricket, and Rummy
sit down to watch their favorite
show on TV.

"I could do better than that," said Rattle.

"Well, I could do better than *you* could," replied Ricket.

"Oh, really? *I* could do better than *you* think you could do when
you're trying to do better than I could!" said Rattle with a snort.

"Ha! *I* can definitely do even better than THAT, although you
THINK you could do better than I can do better!" shouted Ricket.

Rattle knew there was only one way to settle their argument.

"I challenge *you* to a spell-casting contest!" she cried.

"*Tongue of toad
and drool of dog,
Turn this witch
into a frog!*"
Ricket chanted.

Poof!

(Well, at least
Rattle turned green.)

"Eye of bat and black squid's ink,
Make my sister start to shrink,"
chanted Rattle.

But Ricket began to blow up
like a balloon and then took
off around the room.

Pop!
Hissss sssssssssss

Ricket finally landed in a heap on her chair.
Glaring at Rattle, she chanted,

**"Claw of crab and weasel's ear,
Make my sister disappear."**

Pfufffff!

Moments later Rattle disappeared,
and Ricket gave a triumphant cackle.

(Ricket is good . . .
but not that good.
Rattle hadn't disappeared.
She was clinging to the
top of a nearby flagpole!)

"Legs of spiders…"

"shell of snails…"

The witches carried on, and the spells flew back and forth.

"Firefly's wings, and wombats' tails..."

"legs of bugs, and trails of slugs..."

"Aaaahh . . ."

"... aaaaaahhhhhhhhhhhhh!"

"Where's Rummy?" cried Rattle.

One spell had gone very, very wrong.
Rummy was now disappearing down
the road in the back of a garbage truck—
among the snails, bugs, and slugs!

Rattle jumped onto her
broomstick and flew out
the window in pursuit
of the garbage truck.

(And Ricket? Well, she was struggling
to get airborne.)

Just as the witches were
catching up to the
garbage truck,
the wind

blew Rattle off
her broomstick.

She tumbled through
the air, landing
with a loud bump
on the windshield of
the garbage truck,
which came to a stop.
Overjoyed, the two witches hugged
Rummy—

but not too close, because he smelled
like garbage!

Rattle, Ricket, and Rummy climbed onto Rattle's broomstick and flew home.

And to celebrate,
they decided to
have a party!

So now we're back where we started,
with Rattle
(who clears the dance floor)

and Ricket
(who clears the plates)

and Rummy . . .

who just clears up the mess!